Vanessa-Fei

The Girl Who Could Touch the Sky

WANDERS THE WORLD!

VOLUME I

GRACE FAITH HOPE

Juanita McCarter Bryan

To order additional copies of this book, contact:
Xlibris
844-714-8691
www.Xlibris.com
Orders@Xlibris.com

ISBN: Softcover   978-1-6698-6493-6
         Hardcover   978-1-6698-6494-3
         EBook   978-1-6698-6492-9

Print information available on the last page

Rev. date: 02/28/2023

Vanessa-Fei

The Girl Who Could Touch the Sky

WANDERS THE WORLD!

VOLUME I

GRACE   FAITH   HOPE

Juanita McCarter Bryan

Hebrews 13:16: "And do not forget to do good and to share with others, for with such sacrifices God is pleased."

Dedicated to my extremely smart and adventurous grandson, Ellison.

Expressing much gratitude to my dear daughter, Natasha Rodgers, for her helpful input from a child's perspective.

To my dear friend, Natasha Foreman; Thank you again for the fantastic editing! You are the best!

To my loving and supportive husband, Claude; Thanks for believing in me.

To my parents, thank you for your unconditional love!

To the children reading this book, you are loved. Remember to dream big! Anything is possible.

Vanessa-Fei came upon a sidewalk lined with stars. As she got closer, she noticed there was one with Mickey Mouse's name on it. Excited to see this, she stopped to take a closer look.

She was so distracted by all the stars that she did not notice the girl running very fast towards her.

Not paying attention, the girl bumped right into Vanessa-Fei. The two of them fall to the ground.

"HEY," shouted the girl, "WATCH WHERE YOU ARE GOING!!"

Vanessa-Fei looked up as the girl stood up and began to run away.

"Wait! Where are you going?" Called out Vanessa-Fei.

"HURRY, WE MUST GO NOW!" said the girl!

Vanessa-Fei followed the girl into an ice cream shop.

"Mmmmmm, I want some ice cream; how about you?" asked the girl.

"That would be nice!" said Vanessa-Fei.

The girl reached into her backpack and pulled out a handful of money to pay for their ice cream.

Vanessa-Fei had never seen so much money.

"Where did you get all that money?" asked Vanessa-Fei.

"Don't worry about that. What is your name?" the girl responded.

"My name is Vanessa-Fei! What's yours?"

Before the girl could answer, a boy enters the ice cream shop with his parents and screams, "Hey mom, Hey dad, that's Zoe St. John, the movie star!"

"Can I have your autograph?"

The little girl grabbed Vanessa-Fei by the arm, and they ran out of the shop.

"Hey, are you really a movie star?" asked Vanessa-Fei. The girl did not respond but instead led Vanessa-Fei over to a star with the name, "Zoe St. John" written on it. She pointed to the star and said, "that's me!" Vanessa-Fei was amazed!

The girls head for Zoe's home.

Zoe's mother, Mrs. St. John, met them at the door. She was very angry...."WHERE HAVE YOU BEEN, ZOE? I HAVE BEEN WORRIED SICK ABOUT YOU! WE ARE LATE AGAIN FOR THE STUDIO!"

Zoe's father, Mr. St. John, said, "Why don't you give her a break? You are too hard on her!"

Ignoring Vanessa-Fei, the mother shouted, "ZOE GO TO YOUR ROOM AND GET READY TO LEAVE!"

Zoe looked at her mother, and without hesitation, she said aloud and confidently, "NO!"

The front door opens, and in walks a tall sweaty out-of-breath man who has just spent most of the morning looking for Zoe. Vanessa-Fei learns that this man is Zoe's agent.

He says, "I am getting sick and tired of playing these games and chasing after her when she runs away!"

Zoe says, "you are getting paid very well, so you will do whatever I want you to do!"

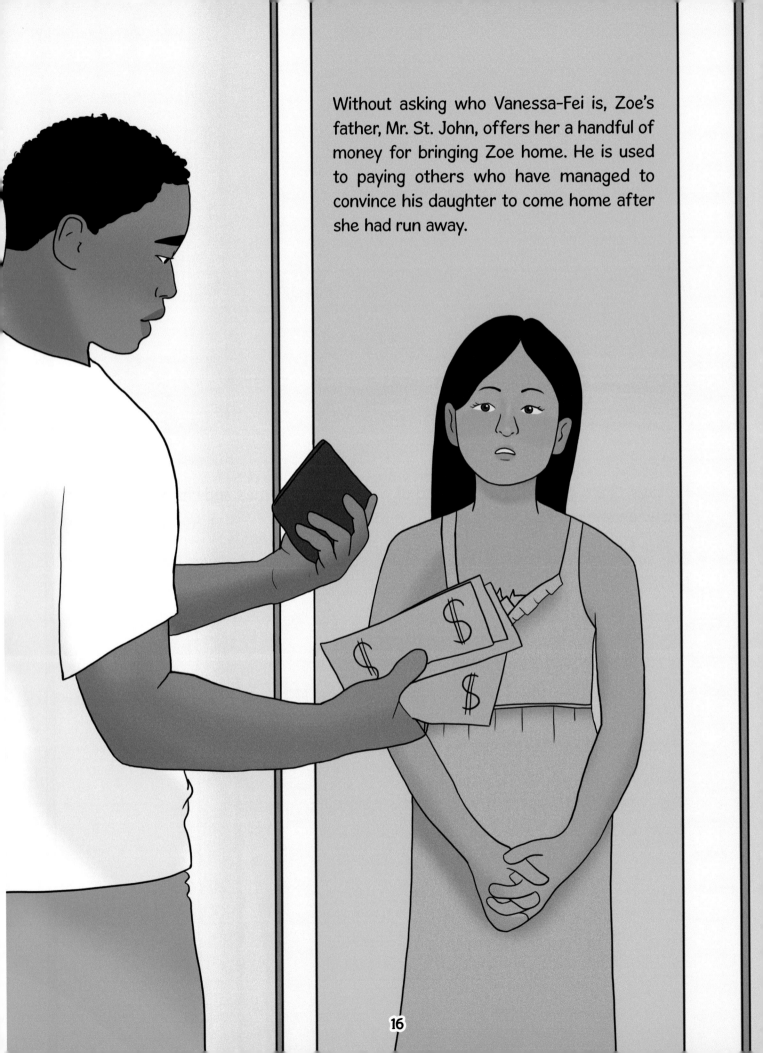

Without asking who Vanessa-Fei is, Zoe's father, Mr. St. John, offers her a handful of money for bringing Zoe home. He is used to paying others who have managed to convince his daughter to come home after she had run away.

Vanessa-Fei says, "no sir, I cannot take your money."

Mr. St. John says, "Ok, if you will not take the money, please stay for lunch."

Watching Zoe and her parents interact, Vanessa-Fei realizes that Zoe has everything she ever wanted but not what she needs. She longs to be a normal kid; A kid who has friends who like her not only because she is famous or rich-- real friends, a kid who can go to a public school like other kids, and parents who do not push her so hard to make movies.

After a nice lunch, Zoe and Vanessa-Fei walk toward the door. Once outside Vanessa-Fei notices a girl on the driveway near the garage playing with an old bicycle. Zoe yells at her, saying, "Didn't I tell you to throw that old bike away! I am getting a new one!"

The girl says, "Yes, but nothing is wrong with it; it is just a little rusty. I can clean it up and ride it to school. Please, can I keep it?"

Zoe screamed, "I don't care. I told you to throw it away! Now do it!"

The girl cries, saying, "I wish you wouldn't be so mean to me all the time."

Vanessa-Fei was shocked and felt bad for the girl. You see, Rachel and her mom has lived with Zoe and her parents since Rachel was an infant. Her mom worked for the family for almost 10 years before Rachel was born.

Zoe's mother called for both girls and asked Vanessa-Fei if she would like to go along with them to the studio. Vanessa-Fei says, "yes," as she has never been to a studio before.

At the studio, Zoe is met by her producer, who shows her the script and reviews what she will be doing in the movie. Instantly, Zoe yells, "I Don't Want This Part. I want the other part in the movie!"

The producer says, "Zoe, we talked about this before, and I asked you if you wanted the other part, and you said no, so we gave it to another girl. At this point, we cannot take it from her. It would not be nice."

Zoe says, "I don't care! I can do whatever I want because I make the money that pays you."

"If I don't get that part, I won't do it at all!" Then she storms out the door.

Mrs. St. John tries to convince the producer to change his mind. But he says, "I won't do it. I can't hurt the other girl like that. This is not the first time Zoe has done this, making us run late! I will not do it this time!"

Mrs. St. John runs after her daughter. This time Zoe is disrespectful to her mother in front of everyone.

Vanessa-Fei is very calm and does not let Zoe's outbursts bother her, but she does not like how Zoe speaks to her mother.

Hollywood Hall of Fame

Dorothy Dandridge

Marilyn Monroe

Zoe St. John

Audrey Hepburn

Diahann Carroll

Vanessa-Fei and the other girl walk around admiring all the movie stars on the wall. There was even a nice picture of Zoe!

The girls were also excited to see all the people busy running around the studio.

"What is your name?" asks Vanessa-Fei. "My name is Rachel." "It is very nice to meet you, Rachel! I am Vanessa-Fei!"

Rachel tells Vanessa-Fei how much she admires Zoe even though she is mean to her. She wishes she could trade places with her because she has so many pretty dresses and lots of toys.

Hollywood Hall of Fame

Dorothy Dandridge

Marilyn Monroe

Zoe St. John

Audrey Hepburn

Diahann Carroll

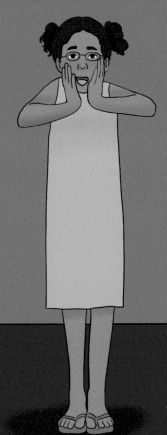

"Where is Zoe? We are losing money!" shouts the producer.

Frustrated with Zoe, the producer sees the girls talking and walks toward them. He is particularly interested in Rachel, who looks Zoe's age and size. He asks her if she wants to be in a movie. Rachel is very excited and screams, "YES, I would love to be in a movie!"

Vanessa-Fei watches as Rachel reads the script and gives her a thumbs-up!

After she finishes, the film crew says how much they love her and how nice she is to them.

Vanessa-Fei overhears a group of people saying they only tolerate Zoe because she is famous and rich. She is always slowing down production with her bad attitude.

After several hours, Zoe and her mom returned to the studio. The producer tells Zoe's mom that they are dropping Zoe from the movie and that they have found a new girl with just as much talent as Zoe but a lot nicer.

When the mother asked who was taking Zoe's place, the producer pointed to Rachel, who was still excited.

Later when they get back to Zoe's house, Rachel jumps out of the car and runs as fast as she can to her mother to tell her the good news! Rachel's mother is so excited, and they both scream and jump up and down!

Zoe walks past them and goes straight upstairs to her room without saying a word.

Zoe's mother approaches Rachel's mother. She says, "I understand if you want to quit your job as our housekeeper now that your daughter will become a movie star."

Rachel's mom responded, "no, ma'am, I want to continue working here. You are my family, and I like what I do. Besides, I do not want to depend on my daughter's money. I want to make my own money."

Zoe's mother looks puzzled.

Mrs. St. John added, "Zoe used to be a good kid before she became a famous movie star. It seems that suddenly, she wasn't our kid anymore." She says, "I hope Rachel does not change."

As Rachel goes over her script in her bedroom, Vanessa-Fei looks at her and says, "You know, Zoe could use a good friend right now. You can be that friend."

"Yeah, but she has never wanted to be my friend," says Rachel.

"Being kind to a friend is easy. Being kind to an enemy takes effort. Who knows, you may end up with a real friend. Give it some thought," says Vanessa-Fei.

The next day at the studio, Rachel went into the producer's office to talk with him before she started work. "Would you please give Zoe a part in the movie?" The producer said, "but why? She is so mean to you and everyone else."

Rachel said, "I think she will be nicer now, and besides, she is my friend. Can you please just give her another chance?"

Because of Rachel, the producer decides to give Zoe a small part in the movie.

Zoe was happy when her mother told her that she would get a small part in the movie. She was happy because she really loves acting a lot. She just did not like being a kid star with all the responsibilities of an adult.

Zoe learned a big lesson from Rachel about friendship and being polite to others. She thanked Rachel for being a good friend and then asked for her autograph. They both laughed. "Friends for life!" says Zoe.

"Friends for life!" says Rachel.

Both girls smile and hug each other.

Discuss with your parents:

What does kindness mean to you? _____

_____

Why is it important to be kind to others? _____

_____

What are 2 ways you can show kindness to yourself and others?

1. _____

2. _____

What lesson did Zoe learn from Rachel? _____

_____

What lesson did Zoe's mother learn from Rachel's mother?

_____

Do you know what city and state Vanessa-Fei is visiting?

_____

What are the clues/landmarks in the story that helped you guess correctly?

_____

Have you visited this city/state? _____ Yes _____ No

If so, Vanessa-Fei would love to see your pics! Have your parents add a pic of your family visit to her Instagram page: @vanessafei38

Hope you enjoyed reading this book!

Stay tuned for other adventures and stories as Vanessa-Fei Wanders the World!

Printed in the United States
by Baker & Taylor Publisher Services